Tale of the Scorpion King

Also by Nicole Lisena Landsman

A Knight's Fairytale

Tale of the Scorpion King

By

Nicole Lisena Landsman

Illustrated by

Alanna Johnson

For my loving husband.

Thank you for everything. I love you.

Once upon a time there was a King named James who lived in a faraway land of green rolling hills and magnificent purple mountain ranges. His castle was made of the finest granite taken from those mountains with ribbons of green, black, and white dancing throughout the stone. It was perched on the tallest hill overlooking a lake with the most crystal blue water ever seen.

King James ruled his kingdom with an iron fist. He was quite strict with his laws and insisted his subjects follow them to the letter. Punishment was swift and harsh for those that broke the cannons of the realm. Many of his vassals lived in fear of his wrath. There were rumors of the King's dungeon being filled with horrible creatures that would eat a person alive.

Most people imprisoned there were never seen or heard from again.

In this kingdom there lived a young, but powerful witch named Helena. She mostly kept to herself brewing potions and performing small charms and spells for the town's people, but she loved a young man who worked for the King. His name was Ian, and as a craftsman could work equally well with stone, glass, wood, or metal. His creations were exquisite to behold. The witch and the craftsman loved each other very much and were making plans to marry.

One day King James demanded Ian create for him a work of art more intrictate and beautiful than anything the craftsman had yet created. "I command you to make for me a crystal dragon. It must breathe fire."

"Yes, Your Majesty," replied Ian.

Ian slaved over the hot furnace working his magic on the glass to draw forth the dragon. After two days and nights of back-breaking, sweaty labor, Ian presented the King with a sculpture so realistic it seemed as though it may take flight. It truly was a thing of beauty. The King, however, was not pleased.

"This is completely unsatisfactory!" bellowed King James. "You will remake it bigger and better. And

don't forget to destroy this piece of garbage!" he thundered.

"Yes, Your Majesty," said Ian.

Rather than destroy the dragon he had just created he decided to keep it to give to Helena as a wedding gift because he knew *she* would love it. However, this was against the laws of the kingdom. King James had decreed out of jealousy any object the King orders to be destroyed cannot be kept or given to another; but Ian wasn't thinking about the rules. He was only thinking of how much he loved Helena and how much she would love the crystal dragon.

When the King learned Ian didn't destroy the sculpture he became furious.

"How dare you disobey the laws of this land? You are hereby charged with treason to the crown and sentenced to death! The execution will take place in the town square at noon tomorrow!"

Ian was beheaded in public as a lesson to the rest of the domain lest any of them dare to betray him ever again. Helena was distraught and inconsolable over the loss of her beloved. In her grief she cursed King James with a dark and powerful spell.

"Curse you!" she yelled. "He was a sweet and loving man who never had a malicious thought or brought harm to another soul. He broke your stupid law out of love, not revenge. If you ever loved someone you would understand. May you spend the rest of your miserable life as the monster you really are at heart!" she spat at him.

Enraged by the witch's actions, King James became the monster he was cursed to be, a great poisonous scorpion. His fury led him to kill off half the citizens of the territory before he sought the quiet and solace of his own castle.

After that day the people of the realm were more afraid of what the King would do to anyone who broke the laws of the land than ever before. The rumors of the monster grew and grew until they reached beyond the borders of the kingdom. The events of that day became a legend that was altered and distorted with each telling, until the truth became warped and the story took on a life of its own.

The tale reached a faraway land where there lived a princess who dreamed of exploration and battle. She had no interest in what she thought was a boring life at court and she would much rather be out riding her horse through the forest near her home looking for adventure.

Princess Adara was quite skilled with a blade and had no equal when it came to a bow. However, because she was a princess it was frowned upon for her to venture too far from the safety of her father's castle.

"That isn't how a proper lady should behave," said her father, King Philip.

"I don't want to be a proper lady; being bored and cooped up in a castle all day. I want to feel the wind on my face and excitement in my soul," she replied. So she practiced with her sword and her bow as she pretended to fight off the monsters of the wild.

King James wanted to have the curse removed. His servants were terrified of him and left him for safer work. He had heard the myths and tales of a wizard who lived like a hermit in a dark forest, so one day he set out on a journey to find this wizard and demand his help in breaking the spell. The King travelled far and wide looking for the old hermit but to no avail. He came across all manner of creatures on his quest but none would help him.

The Dwarves he found cared nothing for his troubles and told him to leave their lands. King James became furrious with them for not helping and turned into the wicked scorpion. He attacked their stronghold but the Dwarves retreated to the security of their mountain leaving the monster to fruitlessly attack the solid rock. Finally, after his anger subsided, King James returned to himself and continued his search.

Along his travels King James came to the land of the Fairie Folk, but they were wary of strangers and 6never showed themselves. They remained hidden even when the King pleaded for their help. When the scorpion showed itself, they were happy with their decision to remain undisclosed.

In the territory of the Centaurs, King James tried to demand help but they only wanted to be left alone and when the King refused to leave their domain the centaurs attacked. In his rage the King transformed into the monster and a fierce battle ensued. Many Centaurs were killed either by the scoprion's poisonous sting or its great pincers; the few remaining survivors retreated. Because of his armor-plated shell the King wasn't injured at all.

With each realm King James travelled through word spread and the story and rumors grew. Princess Adara was enthralled by the tales she heard from visitors to the castle. She yearned for more than just stories and imagined what she would do if the great monster ever came within the borders of her land. Her father worried about her safety.

"I don't want you to wander outside alone. You are to stay within the confines of the town gates," said King Philip.

"That's not fair!" cried the princess. "You can't keep me locked up like a prisoner!"

"It's for your own protection."

"I can protect myself. I'm not helpless."

"Okay, but you are not to go beyond the boundaries of the kingdom," her father told her. "Give me your word."

"I promise," she replied with a sigh.

As she wandered out for her daily ride she thought about the wild stories of the monstrous scorpion. *He can't be all bad,* she thought to herself. *There must be something good in him. I'm not afraid, not all things are what they seem.*

King James continued to search for the reclusive wizard but with no one to help him he was starting to lose hope of ever getting the curse lifted. He became a sad man all alone with only his horse to keep him company.

One day, after what felt like an eternity of searching, the King finally found what he had been looking for. He glimpsed an old run-down building deep in the heart of a forgotten forest. As he drew near, an ancient little man with snow white hair and beard to match came out of the cottage. His long blue robe swept the ground as he walked. He was an odd little fellow after spending so much time alone; muttering under his breath while he worked his charms and spells mostly speaking to the local animals. Not accustomed to having guests, he was wary of strangers and was about to go back inside upon sight of the King approaching.

"Don't go," called out the King. "Are you the wizard of myth and legend?" he asked.

"I don't know much about any myths or legends, but I am a wizard," the old man replied.

"I am King James and I have travelled far afield and across many miles to find you. I need you to help me," said the King.

"How do you know I will be able to?" asked the wizard. "What is it you need done?"

"I need you to break a curse placed on me by an evil witch."

"Who was this witch and what sort of curse it it?" inquired the old man.

King James was begining to lose his patience. "I don't know just some local witch. She turned me into a monster!" he shouted.

"I must say you don't look very much like a monster," said the conjurer with a smile.

"Not all the time!" yelled the King, his anger bubbling just below the surface. "I'm only a monster sometimes!"

"I see," said the sorcerer who was starting to get an idea of the King's true nature. "Come inside and I will see what I can do."

King James followed the wizard into the cottage. It was a small, thatch roofed stone building so old it was crumbling. There were a few grimy windows leaving the inside dimly lit.

"Touch nothing," said the wizard. "Most things in here are very delicate."

"How long will this take?" demanded the King.

"Things like this can't be rushed. It will take as long as it takes," replied the old man. "Now sit down and touch nothing."

The wizard then set to his work. He checked great tomes of magic looking for anything that might help. He bustled about mixing herbs and powders. He muttered incantations and spells.

The King sat down in the only chair he could find but he was impatient to have the curse broken and kept getting up to pace the tiny cottage. The old man was becoming distracted by all the movement.

"Either sit down or get out. You are disrupting my concentration. Do you want me to attempt to remove the curse or not?"

King James was not in the habit of being spoken to in such a manner.

"How dare you address me in that tone of voice? I am a King and deserve your respect!" he yelled.

"You came to me remember? If you want my help you will sit down and keep quiet or I will turn you into a toad and feed you to the snakes in the forest!" the wizard yelled back.

The King's temper finally got the better of him. He turned into the scorpion and attacked the old man. The wizard quickly cast a spell to relocate himself out of danger before the creature could strike him. In his rampage King James upset some unstable experiments

and blew up half the cottage and nearly destroyed himself as well.

Having seen the effects of the curse which had been placed upon the King, the wizard reappeared and said, "I can't help you, but there is someone who mights be able to. There is a healer in a distant land who could possibly be of assistance. Ride into the setting sun for three weeks. You will come to a wide river than can only be crossed on the night of the full moon. Once across, turn and follow the river through the mountains. On the other side in a valley you will find the land of which I speak. Ask for Agnes the healer. Perhaps she can help. Oh, and during your travels I suggest you work on controlling you temper." With those final words the wizard disappeared leaving the scorpion alone in the forest.

After his fury had run its course the King returned to his human form. He started to follow the path the old man had laid before him.. As King James made his way out of the forest and toward the mighty river he thought about how his anger causes him to change into the great monster. At first he felt the problem wasn't with him but with everyone else around him. *Am I not entitled to feel anger? If other people have a problem with it they can just stay away,* he thought.

I don't want people bothering me anyway. How dare that witch cast a spell on me? I am the King!

As he continued his journey to find the healer, King James occasionally felt lonely for some human interaction. His horse was his companion, but sometimes it wasn't enough. He longed for the company of other humans. This sometimes made him sad. *Who would want to be friends with a monster?* The king felt he was destined to be alone for the rest of his life.

As Princess Adara took her daily ride she longed for advventure. She wanted more from life than to spend it day after day in her father's court. She wanted someone to love her and treat her as an equal not as a prized possession or a delicate object, even worse as an inferior woman. She wanted excitement and new possibilities. The princess started to take longer rides farther and farther from her father's castle. She thought she could handle any danger that might cross her path and so she felt justified in taking longer rides pushing the edges of her promise, but she was always careful to stay within the boundaries of the kingdom.

One day as she was out practicing her bow, Adara came across a stranger riding through the woods. He was strikingly heandsome but appeared to be very sad.

"Hello," she called to him.

The stranger looked around surprised to come across another human being.

"Hello," he called back to her.

"I'm sorry if I startled you. I didn't mean to scare you."

"It's okay. I guess I was just lost in thought."

"I can see that. They must be very deep thoughts to distract you so," she said.

"Actually, they are."

"Anything I can help you with?" she offered.

"That depends," the stranger replied. "Who are you and where do you come from?" he asked.

"My name is Adara and I live in this realm," she answered. "Does that help you?"

"Maybe. My name is James."

"It's nice to meet you, James. Where are you from?" she inquired.

"I come from a land very far away. It feels like I have been traveling for an eternity."

"You must be exhausted. There is a kingdom a few miles from here. I'm sure you could find food and rest there."

"Thank you. I would like that. How is it you are out here all alone with no one to protect you?" he asked.

"I'm perfectly capable of protecting myself, thank you," she replied a little more forcefully than she meant to. "I'm sorry. I just don't like it when people think I can't handle myself because I happen to be female."

"I'm sorry. I didn't mean to offend you," said James. "Are you any good with that?" he asked pointing to her bow.

"Maybe," she answered playfully.

James was intrigued by Adara's nature. He had never encountered anyone like her. She was very beautiful and she was also unafraid to speak her mind. The more they talked he realized she was smart, funny, and curious about everything; and he was totally captivated by her eyes which he thought sparkled like diamonds.

Always looking for news of the world beyond the borders of her father's kingdom Adara asked James to tell her about his travels. She couldn't believe all the places he had been! She was never allowed to go anywhere and she longed to see past the horizon. His stories were interesting and she found he was a great story teller but she couldn't quite put her finger on what was making him seem so sad. She sensed he was leaving something out.

As the two of them walked through the forest towards the kingdom they talked a great deal.

"I enjoyed our walk and I would love to see you again, perhaps tomorrow," said Adara.

"I too enjoyed our time together. It is nice to have some company for a change. Do you ride out every day?"

"Yes I do," she replied.

"Then I shall look forward to tomorrow," said James.

The guards saluted as they approached the gates. Adara stopped once they were inside the walls.

"We must part ways here I'm afraid," she said. "But we will meet in the forest tomorrow. I hope you find what you are seeking. Good-bye."

James was sad to see her go but he felt better than he had in a long time. He thought if he could only get the curse removed perhaps there might be a future for him and Adara. With a small spark of hope he went in search of the healer, Agnes.

Adara headed for her father's castle thinking about her time spent with James. She really *had* enjoyed his company. He had started to treat her as an equal and not just some woman and because she didn't tell him she was a Princess he also didn't bow down to her and try to turn her into an object meant to be looked at in a glass case. She was looking forward to her ride the next day.

"There you are," said her father, King Philip. "Where were you?"

"I was out for my ride just like any other day. Why?"

"I have some news to tell you. Some very important guests will be arriving and we will be hosting a tournament in their honor."

"I wish to compete in the games!" she said excitedly. "I have been practicing every day."

"You most certainly will not compete! As the princess for this kingdom you will behave like a proper lady. I will have none of your foolishness. That is my final word on the matter."

"Can I still take my daily ride if I promise to behave?" she asked.

"Okay, but you must stay within the borders and I expect you to keep your promise to behave."

"I will," she replied happily.

The next day James went to find Agnes. He found her place tucked in a quiet corner of the kingdom. It was a small, unassuming building with a wooden sign depicting a mortar and pestle hanging above the door. Inside it was well kept. The floors were clean and well-polished. The walls were covered in shelves that were filled with books on all sorts of topics from boils and rashes to broken bones and fevers. Everything was in its place and neat.

As James entered a woman called out from the back, "I will be right with you."

A few minutes later a small plump woman with her brown hair pulled up into a bun and wearing an apron came out from behind a red velvet curtain that separated the living quarters from the rest of the space.

"How may I help you?" she asked.

"I have travelled the four corners of the world searching for someone to help me break a curse placed upon me by a witch. I was told you could help me," said James.

"Perhaps, but first I need to know a little bit about the curse. What are its effects?"

"I am cursed to be a monster for the rest of my life. Please, you must help me," he replied.

"Well, since you don't look like a monster at the moment I would guess it happens only at certain times; for example when the moon is full or when the sun goes down. Is that true?"

"Yes, I become the monster when I get angry."

"What sort of monster do you transform into?" asked Agnes.

A giant scorpion with a poisonous sting," said James.

"I can't help you today, but give me a week to do some research and maybe then I will be able to help you."

"A week!" exclaimed James, who was starting to feel his anger rise. "I can't wait a week! The monster could show up before then. You don't understand.

There is a young woman I met and I think I love her. She is the one person in this world who doesn't hate or fear me. Please, you must help me," he begged.

"I'm sorry," Agnes said calmly. "I need to prepare. I don't want to harm you accidently by not knowing what I am doing. Please try to control your anger until then."

James left the healer's place feeling very disappointed and worried. He was supposed to go riding with Adara but he was concerned he wouldn't be able to control the monster. With a heavy heart he set out for the forest to meet with her. As he entered the lush green woods he caught sight of her and his mood lifted.

"Hello," he called out to her.

"Hello," she said with a smile as she reigned in her horse. "I'm delighted to see you."

"I'm happy to see you too," he smiled back. "I see you brought your bow with you again. Are you going to show me how good you are?" he asked playfully.

"Perhaps," she said with a grin. "Actually there is to be a tournament next week. Will you be staying to compete?"

"As it turns out I have business keeping me here until then, but I don't know about competing."

"We could see each other every day. I could help you practice if you like. I have a fair amount of skill," she said as she fingered her bow.

"Maybe," replied James. "You might convince me if you show me an example of your talent first."

Adara smiled at him as she fitted an arrow. She had many targets placed throughout the woods and she chose one that was located in a tree quite a distance away. She released the bow string with a twang and her arrow shot through the air and hit the target squarely in the center with a solid thump.

"Wow, that is impressive!" exclaimed James. "You are exceptionaly good."

"Thank you," she replied with a curtsy. "I'm glad you think so. I have worked very hard to become so. What do you think of competeing now?"

"Will you be one of the contestants?"

"I will not be allowed to compete unfortunately. My father forbids it," she said sadly.

"In that case I will enter the competition," James said hoping to make her smile. "Perhaps, if you practice with me I may even win."

"I would gladly practice with you every day until the tournament," she replied her mood brightening. "We can work each day on a different event. We can start with the bow and arrow today."

"I would like that. Please, begin. I am ready whenever you are."

All day Adara and James worked together challenging one another to farther and more difficult targets and enjoying the companionship.

"You have improved greatly today," said Adara as they walked back towards the town gates.

"Thank you. It is due to your instruction. You are a wonderful teacher."

"Thank you. I had a really enjoyable day. I hope you did too."

"I did and I look forward to tomorrow."

"So do I, James."

All week Adara and James worked together in the forest. They practiced with the sword, the bow, and of course the joust.

"I think you are well prepared, James. Good luck tomorrow," said Adara as she quickly kissed him.

"Th-th-thank you," he stuttered in surprise, his eyes wide. "I hope I won't disappoint you. You have been a wonderful teacher."

"I have been so happy this past week. Life can be so lonely and it is nice to be able to share the things I love with someone."

"I agree it is nice to have someone to share life with."

"Until tomorrow then," she said as they parted just inside the gates.

"Until tomorrow," he replied.

Agnes searched through every book she could find to look for a cure for King James's curse. She found nothing that would cure him. She had no choice but to admit defeat. The spell the witch had placed on James was too powerful for her to remove. His only options were to live with the curse or ask Helena to remove it. Sadly, Agnes summoned James to her cottage.

"Have you found a way to remove the curse?" James asked hopefully.

"I am sorry, but I have not."

"What? I am a King, I can't live the rest of my life as a monster!" he yelled starting to turn angry.

"I am truly sorry but the spell is too powerful. I am merely a healer and it is beyond my skill to reverse it."

"The wizard said you would be able to help me! Now do something to make it right!" he hollared beginning to lose control.

"You must learn to master you anger. You control the monster; don't let it control you."

James walked away, slamming the door behind him, before the monster could overtake him. It was the first time he had done something positive with his anger. Agnes felt sorry for him as he watched him depart; but she also felt he wasn't a lost cause and there may be hope for him yet.

The day of the tournament dawned clear and bright. The sun was shining high in a deep azure sky and a delightfully cool breeze was blowing through the town carrying with it the tantalizing scent of roasting meat. The whole kingdom was buzzing with excitement. Everywhere there were banners and streamers of every color imaginable hung from windows and doors of merchants and commoners.

The festivities began with a parade through the streets of the kingdom. The competitors astride their horses carried flags with colorful family crests and musicians played a lively tune as the the procession made its way along the streets to the stadium.

The arena was packed with spectators from every corner of the town. The whole kingdom was on holiday to either participate in or watch the tournament. With a great fanfare Adara and her father entered the stadium and were announced. "Everyone please rise for King Philip and Princess Adara!"

King James was surprised to learn Adara was a princess but it did not change his love for her. He wanted her to be his wife; but how could he even begin to think of spending the rest of his life with her if there was no way to remove the curse making him a monster.

King Philip addressed those gathered in the stadium. "Thank you, everyone, for attending this tournament. Competitors, I expect you to play fair and have fun. Good luck!"

The first event of the day was sword fighting. James entered the ring with his opponent. The match started with the clang of a bell and the two contestants came together with the ring of steel on steel as blades

made contact with armor. King James did well, rising through the ranks winning round after round. In the semi-final round he lost a match and ultimately finished in second place.

The next event to take place was the general melee. James was not a very large man, especially compared to his opponents. On the one hand his smaller stature meant he was quicker and lighter on his feet but on the other hand it meant he didn't land as powerful a blow. It was not something James was particularly good at so he only placed fourth.

Archery was the next event. James was very excited about this. He and Princess Adara had worked hard training for this event and he felt very confident in his abilities. She had been a brilliant instructor and he had blossomed under her tutelage.

The targets had been lined up for the contestants at one end of the stadium. The first round was shooting from 25 yards. After the twanging of bow strings the whistling sound of many arrows flying through the air filled the arena. Most of the competitors made the shot easily at this distance.

The next shot was to be from 40 yards. The archers took aim and released their arrows. The shrill whistling sound again filled the air as the many arrows flew towards their targets. James's arrow hit the target dead in the center.

The third and final round was to shoot from 50 yards. It was quite a distance but the king was well prepared. He took a deep calming breath and set his stance. James sighted the target and drew back his arrow. He let go of the bow string and the arrow began its flight. It sailed through the air towards the target and made a perfect bullseye. James was elated to take first place! He knew he owed it all to Adara's patient teaching and hoped he had made her proud.

The joust was the final event and a favorite of the spectators. James chose his lance and mounted his horse. He performed well unhorsing one opponent after another. In the final round of competition on the very last pass his opponent landed the lance squarely in the center of James's chest and knocked him from his mount winding him. James was very upset with himself for losing the match even though he placed second.

With the tournament over the scores were tallied up and given to King Philip. Princess Adara and her father stood to announce the winners. The results were read for each individual event first and the prizes were awarded. Then, the overall results were announced.

"In third place is our very own Sir Liam Graystone," said King Philip. The ovation from the spectators was thunderous. "Well done, Sir Liam! In second place is a royal visitor from a very distant land, King James." There was more ear-splitting applause from the crowd. "Excellent job, King James! In first place, from our neighboring kingdom to the west, is Prince Edward. Congratulations, Prince Edward!" The applause was deafening.

Adara was delighted with how well James had performed, especially in the archery portion of the tournament. He had done well and her heart swelled with love and pride.

King Philip held up his hands to quiet the gathered citizens. "Congratulations to all of the competitors. You performed well and with honor. Please, enjoy the rest of the festivities."

Princess Adara was preparing to personally congratulate King James when her father interupted her thoughts.

"Adara, please come here. There is someone I wish for you to meet. This is Prince Edward; I have arranged for you and him to marry."

"Father, you can't do that!" cried Adara furious.

"You better mind you manners young lady. I am your father and deserve respect."

"But it isn't fair! It is my life! You can't tell me what to do!"

King James was starting to become angry. He felt all of his chances for happiness were fading away.

King Philip was appalled and embarassed at his daughter's behavior. "You listen to me. You will marry Prince Edward and that is the end of the discussion!"

James lost his temper and transformed into the giant poisonous scorpion. Adara tried to intervene but James, blinded by his rage, took no notice of her. He lashed out in anger and stung her with his venomous tail. Everyone stopped what they were doing. James slowly came to his senses and realized what he had done. He ran to her and took her in his arms.

"I'm so sorry, Adara!" he cried. "I never wanted to hurt you. Please, someone help her!" he yelled to the gathering crowd.

Agnes the healer pushed her way through the multitude to the center. She bent over Adara and went to work right away.

"Everyone back up and give me some room."

"Please, help her. You must save her. I love her," pleaded James.

"I will do all I can for her but you must let me do my job."

Agnes mixed herbs and made a dressing for the wound. She sucked out as much of the poison as she could. A stretcher was made and the Princess was carried back to the castle and placed in her bed to rest.

"Only time will tell if she will be spared," said Agnes. "What she needs now is rest."

"Please I would like to stay. I promise not to disturb her."

"You almost killed her! In fact she may still die! I can't allow you to stay here. Please, leave," commanded King Philip.

"But I love her more than anything," begged King James. "I never meant for her to get hurt. Please let me stay."

King Philip agreed to let James stay in the castle. "Leave Agnes to her work and do not pester her," he told James.

"Please find rooms suitable for our guest," he told his staff. After the incident at the stadium James inspired fear wherever he went. The staff wanted to put him in the dungeon, but instead he was shown to rooms in a mostly unused wing of the castle. The apartment he was given was old but well cared for. The stone floors were clean and polished and tapestries depicting dark creeatures hung on the walls. It was well lit with large windows looking out on the great lake below.

James was guilt stricken by what he had done. Adara was the person he truly loved and who loved him in return. He would rather live the rest of his life as a monster than to live without her. Every day he asked about the Princess; every day there was no change.

Agnes tended to Adara day and night. She extracted more poison, cleaned the wound, changed the dressing and tried to bring down the princess's fever. When the fever finally broke Agnes felt Adara was out of danger and on the mend. When the Princess awoke James was by her side.

"James, you could have killed me. If Agnes hadn't been there things might have turned out quite differently. I love you more than anything but you must learn to conquer the beast within you. Anger is natural but you can't let it control you. Please say you will learn. I will do all I can to help you."

"I think I could do anything with you by my side. Will you marry me?"

"Nothing would give me greater pleasure. I will be happy to marry you!"

The wedding took place as soon as Princess Adara was well. It was a wonderful affair with music, dancing, and tables laden with food. The whole kingdom was invited but James and Adara had eyes only for each other. Never had either of them been so happy. And so they remained for the rest of their days.

The End

Acknowledgments

I would like to express my gratitude to Alanna Johnson for providing the illustrations for this story. I am very appreciative of her talents.

Great thanks to Art Rose, Michael Lisena and Barbara Lisena for proofreading. Also an extra thanks to Art Rose for assistance with editing.